D1450721

THOMAS CRANE PUBLIC LIBRARY

QUINCY MASS

CITY APPROPRIATION

FLIGHT
SPACECRAFT

June Loves

This edition first published in 2002 in the United States of America by Chelsea House
Publishers, a subsidiary of Haights Cross Communications

All rights reserved. No part of this publication may be reproduced or transmitted in any form or
by any means without the written permission of the publisher.

Chelsea House Publishers
1974 Sproul Road, Suite 400
Broomall, PA 19008-0914

The Chelsea House world wide web address is www.chelseahouse.com

Library of Congress Cataloging-in-Publication Data Applied for.
ISBN 0-7910-6558-8

First published in 2000 by
Macmillan Education Australia Pty Ltd
627 Chapel Street, South Yarra, Australia, 3141

Text copyright © June Loves 2000

Edited by Lara Whitehead
Text design by if Design
Cover design by if Design
Page layout by if Design/Raul Diche
Illustrations by Lorenzo Lucia
Printed in Hong Kong

Acknowledgements
The author and the publisher are grateful to the following for permission to reproduce
copyright material:

Cover: Skylab Space Station (centre), courtesy of The Photo Library/NASA/Science Photo
Library; satellite rescue mission (background), courtesy of NASA, supplied by Astrovisuals.

Photographs courtesy of: AAP, pp. 7 (bottom), 24 (top), 26 (right); Australian Picture Library/
Corbis-Bettmann, pp. 6, 7 (top); Australian Picture Library/Leo Meier, p. 5 (right); Australian
Picture Library/UPPA, p. 27; NASA, pp. 2 (right), 4, 10 (top), 18, 19, 28; NASA, supplied by
Astrovisuals, pp. 2–3 (background), 8, 9, 11 (bottom), 15 (bottom), 17, 20, 21 (bottom), 22, 23,
25, 26 (left), 30–1 (background), 32; The Photo Library/NASA/Science Photo Library, p. 16.

While every care has been taken to trace and acknowledge copyright the publishers
tender their apologies for any accidental infringement where copyright has proved
untraceable.

Contents

Travelling in space   4

Early rockets   6

Early space flight   8

The Apollo Lunar Program   10

The space shuttle   12

Space stations   16

Satellites   20

Space probes   25

Future space flight   27

The International Space Station (ISS)   28

Space flight timeline   30

Glossary   31

Index   32

Travelling in space

THROUGHOUT THE CENTURIES, people have been fascinated by the moon and the stars. Many early legends and the first science fiction stories tell of fantastic journeys into space.

Centuries ago, people thought that air stretched all the way to the stars. They did not know that space has no air for humans to breathe. As people learned more about space, they began to see the enormous problems that they would have to overcome before they could travel there.

Although dramatic progress has been made in the development of the airplane, piston and jet aircraft cannot operate in space because they need oxygen from the air to operate their engines. They also need air to create lift so they can fly. There is not enough air in the atmosphere for airplanes to fly above about 25,000 meters (82,000 feet).

A view of Simpson Desert in South Australia from the space shuttle Columbia in 1990.

DISTANCES IN SPACE

Distances in space are too enormous to imagine. Our nearest neighbor is the moon, which is 384,000 kilometers (238,618 miles) away. The sun is 150 million kilometers (93 million miles) from Earth and the nearest star is over 250,000 times further.

THE ROCKET ENGINE

The invention of the rocket engine made the exploration of space possible. A rocket engine is the most powerful of all engines. Rockets can travel in space because they carry the oxygen they need with them. They can produce more power for their size than any other engine and can launch spacecraft upwards at 40,000 kilometers (24,856 miles) per hour. Spacecraft need rocket engines to push them up through the Earth's atmosphere for more than 200 kilometers (125 miles) so they can **orbit** around the Earth.

HOW ROCKETS WORK

If you blow up a balloon and then let it go, the air rushes backward out of the neck and pushes the balloon forward. Inside a rocket, liquid fuel like gasoline burns with oxygen to make hot gases. The gases expand and rush backwards. When this happens the rocket is pushed forward, like a balloon.

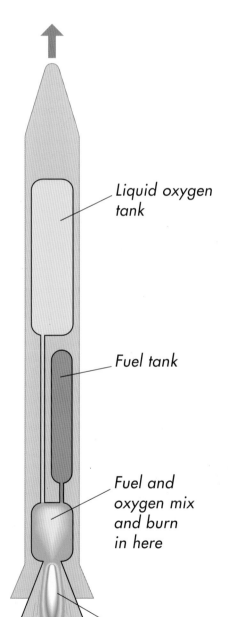

Liquid oxygen tank

Fuel tank

Fuel and oxygen mix and burn in here

A liquid-fuel rocket.

Hot gas rushes out here, pushing the rocket forward

Space Fact

Space is the environment beyond our atmosphere where there is no wind, no air and no sound. Space begins about 100 kilometers (62 miles) above the Earth. The Earth's atmosphere does not exist at this height. Airplanes cannot fly in space, but rocket planes and spacecraft can.

Firework rockets make beautiful, spectacular displays in the sky. They burn fuel in powder form and their slim, pencil shape allows them to fly at high speed through the air.

Early rockets

ROCKETS WERE FIRST launched about 800 years ago. The ancient Chinese used rockets powered by gunpowder as weapons in the early 1200s.

THE MULTI-STAGE ROCKET

Konstantin Tsiolkovsky (1857-1935) was a Soviet school teacher who became known as the 'Father of Space Flight' because of his research in the development of the rocket. Although he did not carry out any experiments with his designs, he realized that to leave the Earth's atmosphere, a multi-stage rocket would be needed. Multi-stage rockets break off in stages, leaving only a small final stage to go into orbit.

THE FIRST LIQUID-FUEL ROCKET

Dr Robert Goddard (1882-1945) was an American who built the first liquid-fuel rocket. In 1926, he launched the world's first rocket that used gasoline and liquid oxygen. The rocket soared to a height of about 55 meters (181 feet). The flight lasted only two and a half seconds. Dr Goddard and his team continued to design bigger, faster rockets until his death in 1945.

Dr Robert Goddard with his first liquid-fuel rocket, 1926.

THE V-2 ROCKET

The German V-2 rocket was the first true rocket. It was one of the most terrifying weapons of World War II, which was fought from 1939 to 1945. Dr Wernher Von Braun (1912-77) and his team of engineers invented the devastating long-range rocket, which could bomb targets over 300 kilometers (186 miles) away. Although the V-2 was a weapon of war, it was a great scientific achievement.

The V-2 was launched vertically from a mobile platform. It could reach a height of 96 kilometers (59 miles), which brought it to the edge of space. By following a high arched path, the missile travelled about 320 kilometers (199 miles) in total.

ROCKETS TO GO TO THE MOON

It was only after World War II that rockets were developed for space flight. The technology behind the V-2 led to the start of space exploration.

After World War II, Dr Wernher Von Braun and his engineers worked with the US government on rocket projects that would enable travel to the moon. Dr Von Braun became the Director of **NASA** in Houston, Texas, and was responsible for the Saturn V rocket that took the Apollo 11 spacecraft to the moon.

Length: 14 meters (45.9 feet)
Weight: 12.2 metric tons (13.4 tons)

A German V-2 rocket.

Dr Wernher Von Braun with his model for a rocket to take men to the moon.

Early space flight

SPUTNIK 1

The Soviet **satellite** Sputnik 1 was launched into orbit on October 4, 1957. Sputnik 1 was a small, 58-centimeter (22.8 inch) aluminum ball weighing 83 kilograms (183 pounds). It orbited 800 kilometers (497 miles) above the Earth. It stayed in orbit for about two months, sending out a small 'beep beep' sound.

SPUTNIK 2

The first living being to travel in space was a dog called Laika. On November 3, 1957, the Soviet Union launched Sputnik 2 with Laika on board. Laika was wired up to relay vital information back to Earth. Unfortunately, Laika died in space when the oxygen ran out. The Sputnik 2 launch paved the way for the first manned space flight, which came four years later in 1961.

ANIMALS IN SPACE

Monkeys and chimpanzees, fruit fly larvae and mice were sent into space before **astronauts**. Monkeys and chimpanzees were the best animals for measuring whether humans could survive in space. They were also intelligent enough to perform basic mechanical tasks in response to flashing lights. The animal space flights proved humans could remain alive and well in space.

This chimpanzee flew on Mercury 2.

THE FIRST MAN IN SPACE

Yuri Gagarin, a Soviet **cosmonaut**, was the first man in space. On April 12, 1961, the Soviet-built Vostok 1 spacecraft launched the capsule that carried Gagarin into space.

Yuri Gagarin made a single orbit of the Earth, then safely parachuted down 108 minutes after take-off. His main job was to observe the automatic systems of the spacecraft, to ensure they were working. Yuri Gagarin became a national hero because of his space flight. He died seven years later in a Mig–15 fighter crash.

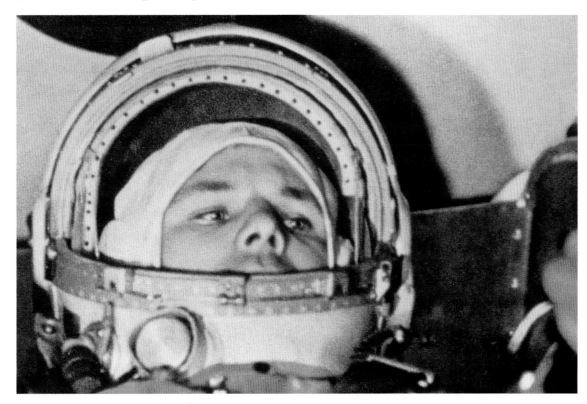

Cosmonaut Yuri Gargarin in Vostok 1.

VOSTOK 1

Early spacecraft such as Vostok 1 were very cramped and uncomfortable. Vostok 1 had a sphere-like capsule that sat on top of an equipment **module**. It contained rockets to control the craft's position and slow it down for re-entry. Vostok 1 travelled at a speed of 28,000 kilometers (17,400 miles) per hour and at a height of 327 kilometers (203 miles) above sea level.

THE FIRST WALK IN SPACE

Later versions of the Vostok spacecraft were called Voskhods. Voskhod 2 was launched in 1965 with a crew of two. One of its crew, Alexei Leonov, made the first walk in space.

Space Fact

In 1963, Vostok 6 carried the first woman, Valentina Tereshkova, into space.

The Apollo Lunar Program

THE US APOLLO LUNAR PROGRAM was a series of expeditions to the moon between 1969 and 1972. It was an important step in the human exploration of space. There were nine expeditions to the moon. Altogether, 12 astronauts have walked on the moon and have carried out many experiments.

The lunar-roving vehicle was driven a total of 35 kilometers (21.7 miles) and many samples of moon rock were collected and returned to Earth.

Astronaut Buzz Aldrin climbing down from the lunar module, July 20, 1969.

THE FIRST MAN ON THE MOON

On July 21, 1969, the American astronaut Neil Armstrong became the first man to walk on the moon when he stepped from the Apollo 11 lunar module. Millions of people on Earth watched on live television as Armstrong stepped onto the moon, saying 'One small step for man, one giant leap for mankind.' Buzz Aldrin followed minutes later. Michael Collins, the third astronaut, remained in orbit.

THE APOLLO 11 SPACECRAFT

The Apollo 11 spacecraft divided into two modules while in orbit around the moon. Armstrong and Aldrin were able to descend to the surface of the moon in the lunar module, while Collins stayed in orbit in the command module. The Apollo spacecraft also had an escape rocket at the top that could lift the command module away from the rocket in an emergency.

SATURN V

The three-stage Saturn V was the most powerful American rocket ever built. It was 110 meters (361 feet) high and was used to launch the various Apollo spacecraft in which astronauts travelled to the moon. It flew 13 times between 1968 and 1973.

Rocket

SPLASHDOWN

The Apollo 11 command module re-entered the Earth's atmosphere at about 39,000 kilometers (24,235 miles) per hour. Parachutes opened to slow it down as it hit the water. Three airbags inflated to keep it upright in the water until US Navy helicopters could winch the crew to safety.

Space Fact

Spacecraft need to fly at a speed of over 40,000 kilometers (24,856 miles) per hour to escape the pull of Earth's **gravity**. This is 20 times faster than Concorde, the fastest jet airliner.

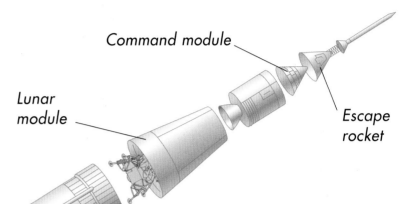

Command module

Lunar module

Escape rocket

The Apollo 11 spacecraft.

Astronaut Allen Shepard on the moon during the Apollo 14 mission.

TEST MISSIONS

A series of space missions were carried out to test the Apollo design. The first flights, Apollo 5 and 6, were unmanned. Apollo 7 took men into Earth's orbit, while Apollo 8 went into lunar orbit. Apollo 9 and 10 tested the lunar module, first around the Earth and then in lunar orbit. Apollo 11 made the first moon landing. There were five more moon landings after Apollo 11.

APOLLO 17

Apollo 17 was the last and longest moon mission. It lasted for 12 days and the astronauts spent 75 hours on the moon's surface.

The space shuttle

THE SPACE SHUTTLE WAS developed by the United States and was the world's first reusable spacecraft. It is a combination of a launcher, a manned spacecraft and an airplane. It can fly people and cargo out of the Earth's atmosphere and into space. Space shuttles were designed to make space flight simpler and cheaper. Before the shuttle, every launch of a spacecraft, **probe** or satellite needed a new rocket.

The cargo bay can carry satellites, scientific and military equipment or a complete space laboratory into space. It is 18.3 meters (60 feet) long and 4.6 meters (15 feet) wide, and can carry loads of up to 29,500 kilograms (64,900 pounds) into low orbit.

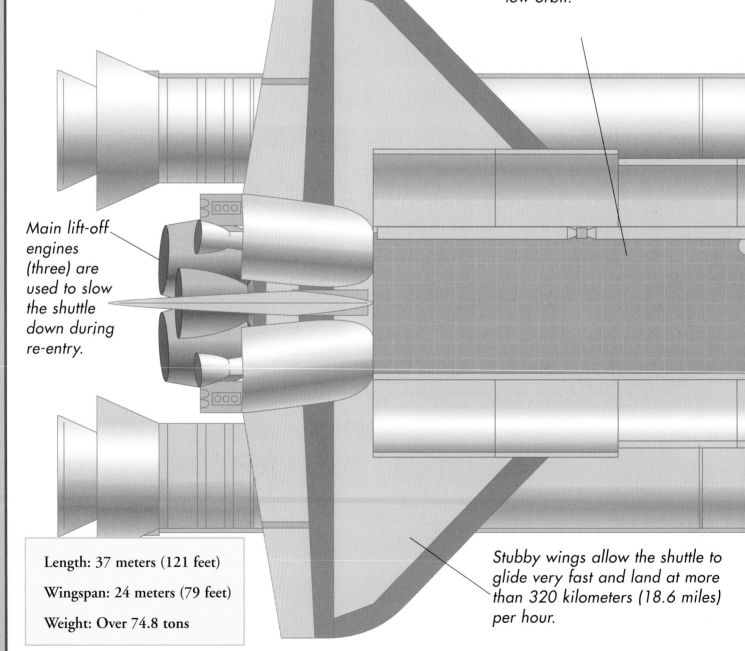

Main lift-off engines (three) are used to slow the shuttle down during re-entry.

Stubby wings allow the shuttle to glide very fast and land at more than 320 kilometers (18.6 miles) per hour.

Length: 37 meters (121 feet)

Wingspan: 24 meters (79 feet)

Weight: Over 74.8 tons

The shuttle lifts off vertically like a rocket and enters space as a spacecraft. When it returns to Earth, it glides down to land on a runway like an aeroplane.

The space shuttle is the size of a jet airliner.

THE ORBITER

The **orbiter** is the part of the space shuttle that looks like an airplane. For take-off, the orbiter is attached to a huge liquid-fuel tank and two smaller solid-fuel **booster** rockets.

 Space Fact

The first space shuttle was the United States' Columbia. It was launched from Cape Canaveral, Florida, in 1981.

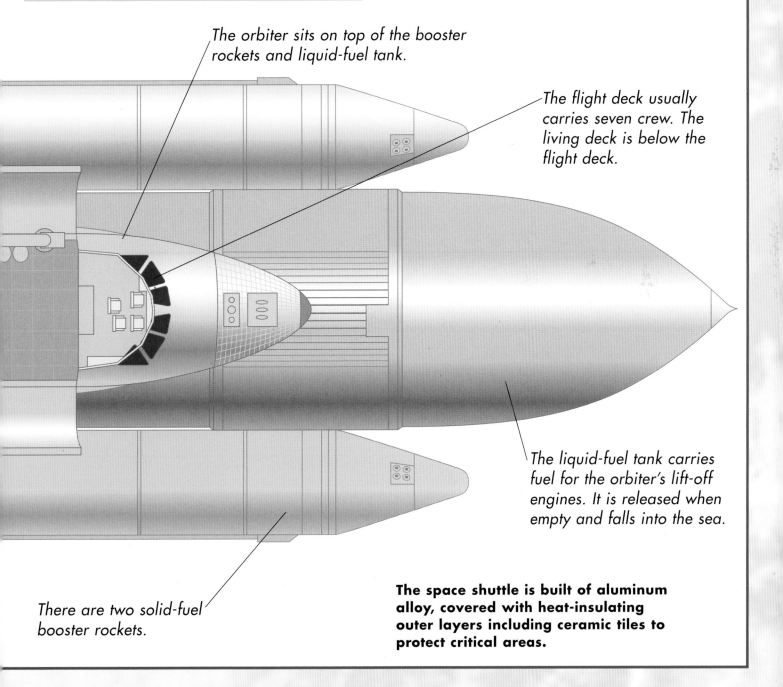

The orbiter sits on top of the booster rockets and liquid-fuel tank.

The flight deck usually carries seven crew. The living deck is below the flight deck.

The liquid-fuel tank carries fuel for the orbiter's lift-off engines. It is released when empty and falls into the sea.

There are two solid-fuel booster rockets.

The space shuttle is built of aluminum alloy, covered with heat-insulating outer layers including ceramic tiles to protect critical areas.

LAUNCH AND RE-ENTRY

Launch and re-entry are the most important parts of a manned flight. The timetable of events leading to a space shuttle launch are called the 'countdown'. All systems such as communications and guidance are checked and rechecked. A space shuttle launch is controlled by the Kennedy Space Center at Cape Canaveral, Florida. Once in orbit, the space shuttle can maneuver, carry out tasks, then re-enter the atmosphere and glide to land on a five-kilometer (3 miles) runway. A space shuttle flight lasts about seven days, although some flights of 30 days are possible. A space shuttle should be capable of 100 missions before it is retired.

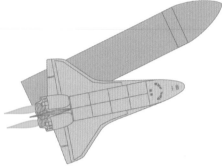

A space shuttle launch

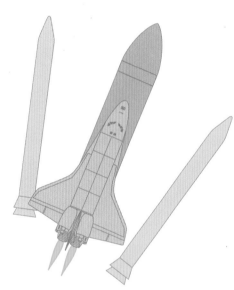

3 **The large external fuel tank breaks away at 110 kilometers (68.4 miles). The tank is released when it is almost empty. It breaks up in the atmosphere and falls into the ocean**

2 **The solid-fuel rockets are released at a height of about 47 kilometers (29.2 miles). The boosters parachute down to Earth and are picked up by a ship.**

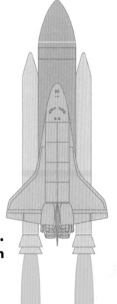

1 **Lift-off! The space shuttle is launched and uses its three main engines plus two solid-fuel rockets. Extra fuel is carried in a huge tank.**

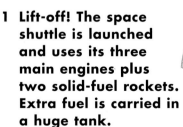

A SPACE SHUTTLE MISSION

Space shuttles are launched regularly to carry out research, conduct experiments in space, and to launch and repair satellites. The shuttle is connected to a huge fuel tank and two rocket boosters when it is launched. The tank carries fuel for the shuttle's engines. The boosters have their own solid fuel and give the **thrust** needed for launch to break through the Earth's atmosphere.

A space shuttle re-entry

1 The orbiter turns around and fires its rocket engines to slow down for re-entry. The orbiter uses its engines and rockets to fly out of orbit and begin the journey down through the atmosphere.

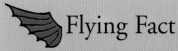 **Flying Fact**

About 31 000 special black and white tiles protect the shuttle from the immense heat as it flies back into the Earth's atmosphere.

2 The orbiter turns around again.

3 Once it is flying at the correct angle, the orbiter continues to fall towards the Earth's atmosphere. The orbiter's tiles absorb the intense heat of re-entry.

4 A few miles from the ground, the undercarriage is lowered and the orbiter slows down.

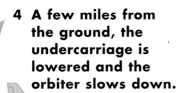

5 The shuttle lands safely on an airforce base runway.

The explosion of the US space shuttle Challenger was the worst space disaster ever. It exploded soon after its launch in 1986 and killed its seven crew members.

15

Space stations

AFTER ASTRONAUTS HAD been to the moon, the next step was to build space stations where astronauts could live while they carried out scientific experiments and research.

SALYUT

The Soviets built the first space station, Salyut 1, in 1971. The first five Salyut stations had only one **docking port**, while Salyut 6 and 7 had two. The addition of a second docking port allowed for the expansion of the station using the Cosmos module. Each Salyut space station was improved and thousands of experiments were carried out during the 14 years of Salyut missions.

SKYLAB

Skylab, the US space station, was put into orbit in February, 1973. There were three missions to Skylab. The first lasted 28 days, the second 59 days and the third 84 days. Each time, the Apollo spacecraft was launched by a Saturn rocket and docked with the space station. Skylab was in orbit for six years, but in use for only six months. It finally fell into the Earth's atmosphere in 1979 and broke up over Australia.

ATLANTIS–MIR

In June, 1995, the US shuttle Atlantis successfully docked with space station Mir. The combined spacecraft held ten people for five days, which included a replacement crew for Mir. Mir's final crew left on August 17, 1999.

The Skylab space station.

MIR SPACE STATION

The Soviet Mir space station was launched in 1986 and was the first permanently manned space station. Since it was launched, it has been continuously occupied with a series of crews sent up in Soyuz spacecraft. Mir is attached at one end to a multi-docking module and at the other to a **propulsion compartment**.

The Mir space station has a special docking unit, which allows a range of other spacecraft such as the Kvant laboratory, the Progress cargo craft and the Soyuz transfer craft to dock with it.

Mir is about 13 meters (42.7 feet) long and 4.5 meters (14.8 feet) in diameter. It consists of two cabins where the crew live. They can make observations through the portholes. Experiments are conducted inside a different module attached to the main section. Large solar panels convert sunlight to electricity.

The Mir space station.

LIVING AND WORKING IN SPACE

Astronauts spend their time working in space carrying out scientific experiments and collecting data from their observations. They also have to do routine housework tasks. Astronauts need air, food, water and waste-disposal systems to survive in space. Air and water are filtered and recycled. Water is a by-product of the shuttle's fuel cells.

DID YOU KNOW?

Some foods found in supermarkets are based on space technology, such as dehydrated meals made up with added water.

Food

On the early space flights, food was squeezed from tubes like toothpaste. Today, new food technology means astronauts enjoy a wide and varied diet similar to food eaten at home. All of their food is carefully weighed and assessed for nutritional value. Astronauts eat from a tray that attaches to their lap or the wall and they use normal utensils. Astronauts drink from containers with straws. Salt and pepper come in liquid form to stop them working their way into the spacecraft's electronics.

Waste in space

In the new International Space Station, wastes that cannot be recycled are returned to Earth for disposal or put in a return vehicle that will burn up on re-entry into the Earth's atmosphere.

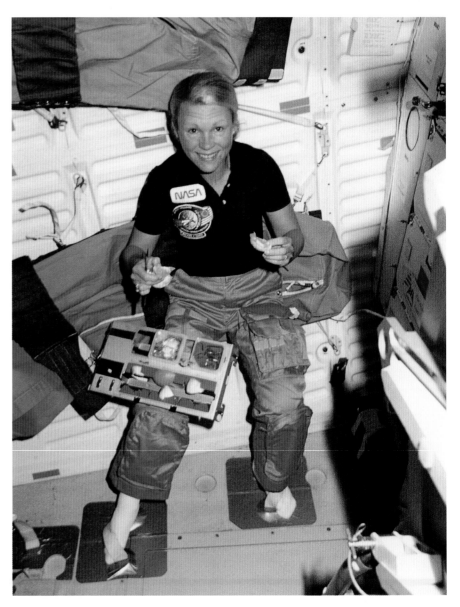

Astronaut Rhea Seddon 'sits' down to a meal in space, 1985.

Sleep

There are no pressure points on the body in a weightless environment. It is easy for the astronauts to make themselves comfortable for sleep in space. They use a sleeping bag attached to a wall, floor or ceiling and drift off to sleep.

Clothes

Inside a shuttle, astronauts wear ordinary clothes with lots of pockets in which to carry things around, and soft shoes.

Moving in space

To move about in space, astronauts wear pressurized space suits, usually with backpacks that contain oxygen and small gas jets. For missions such as recovering and repairing satellites, astronauts can use the manned maneuvering unit (MMU). This is like an armchair that locks onto the back of the space suit. It is equipped with space thrusters that allow the astronaut to move and turn. It also has power outlets and attachment points for lights, cameras and tools.

Astronaut Bruce McCandless using his hands to control his MMU, 1984.

Communication

When astronauts are in space, messages are sent and received constantly. Information from the spacecraft itself is relayed and monitored at mission control. It is important that the mission controllers on the ground know exactly where the spacecraft is, what it is doing and how the crew are feeling. The crew can speak to mission control and send back television pictures. This information is received by ground stations all over the world.

Keeping fit

In space, muscles and bones waste away, blood gets thicker and its volume increases. The spine expands, lengthening the body by two to five centimeters (approximately one to two inches). Astronauts exercise on treadmills and exercise bikes to keep their bodies fit.

Satellites

ARTIFICIAL SPACE SATELLITES ARE unmanned spacecraft that orbit the Earth. They carry out different jobs such as relaying communications and reporting on weather. The modern world depends on satellite technology. Artificial satellites carry large dishes that link countries around the world by relaying vast amounts of information.

SATELLITE ORBITS

Artificial satellites rely on electronic circuits to make them work. Electronic circuits receive and transmit signals and control the satellite in orbit. Today there are hundreds of satellites orbiting the earth. Satellites are placed in different orbits depending on the job they are required to do.

A satellite rescue mission, 1984.

Polar orbit

Satellites in a polar orbit travel above the North and South Poles. They are constantly passing over a different part of the Earth. The polar orbit satellite travels at a height of about 1,000 kilometers (621 miles). They are used for surveillance and sensing satellites.

Geostationary orbit

Satellites in a geostationary orbit travel at a height of 36,800 kilometers (22,868 miles). The satellite orbits at the same rate as the Earth rotates, so it stays above the same spot on Earth all the time. Geostationary orbits are used for communication, broadcasting and navigation satellites.

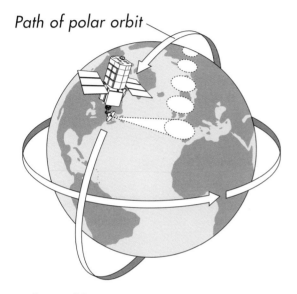

Path of polar orbit

Polar orbit

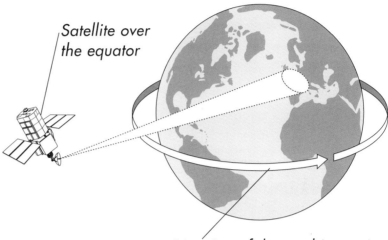

Satellite over the equator

Direction of the earth's rotation

Geostationary orbit

A tracking station in Canberra, Australia picks up signals from orbiting satellites.

TRACKING STATIONS

There is a network of tracking stations set up in different positions around the world. Computers at the tracking stations are used to keep track of artificial satellites and chart their courses.

 Space Fact

The first artificial satellite was the Soviet Union's Sputnik 1, launched in 1957.

TYPES OF SATELLITES

Satellites are vital in our hi-tech world. There are many different types of satellites. Global television and radio, weather maps, long-distance telephone calls, the Internet, ship and airplane navigation and military operations all need satellite technology.

Communication satellites

Most communication satellites, or Comsats, travel on a geostationary orbit far above the equator. They orbit at exactly the same rate as the earth rotates, and always appear to be in the same position over the equator. Because they are in a fixed position, Comsats are used to relay intercontinental telephone calls and live television programs.

Navigation satellites

Navigation satellites enable ships and airplanes with suitable receivers to determine exactly where they are at any time.

Navigation satellites circle the air in a geostationary orbit, giving out signals that are picked up by suitable ground equipment. A crashed airplane's emergency transmitter can send a signal via satellite to ground stations. Using signals from three or more satellites, rescuers can accurately locate the position of the crash.

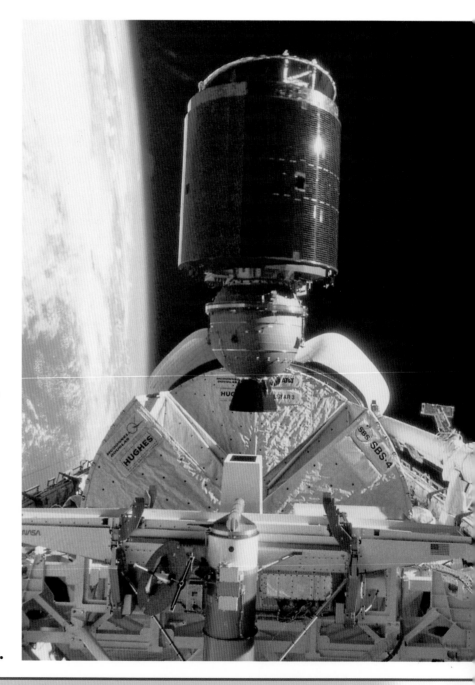

**Space shuttle Discovery
launching three satellites.**

Weather satellites

Weather satellites are important in weather forecasting. They observe our atmosphere from space and help scientists predict the weather. Weather satellites stay in orbit around the Earth for many years and measure land and sea temperatures.

Weather satellites can be used to predict and track the course of storms, hurricanes and tornadoes. Modern weather forecasters can spot danger from pictures taken from the weather satellites and give people adequate warnings.

Earth resources satellites

Earth resources satellites have a bird's eye view of Earth. From a height of hundreds of miles, the Earth can be seen in great detail. Earth resources satellites such as Landsat can observe and record vegetation, air and water pollution, population changes and geological factors such as mineral deposits. Landsat passes over the same part of the Earth's surface every 18 days.

A Landsat photograph of Los Angeles, USA.

Military satellites

Military satellites are used for **reconnaissance**, communications, navigation and electronic intelligence gathering. Some countries launch military satellites to spy on other countries. Spy satellites can observe military targets such as tanks, fighter planes or missiles from low altitudes. They send back detailed pictures to ground stations.

Launching satellites

Rockets are used to launch satellites and space probes into space. Satellites can also be launched from a space shuttle's **payload** bay.

Rocket launches

A rocket-powered launcher must have enough speed to escape Earth's gravity. It is used only once and then jettisoned in space.

A method called 'staging' is used to launch satellites. Three rocket stages are enough to reach space. Each stage falls away as it runs out of fuel, leaving a lighter rocket to fly higher. Strap-on fuel boosters may be used as part of the first stage. They provide extra power during the first part of the flight when the pull of gravity is strongest. The third stage carries the payload and delivers it to orbiting height.

Ariane rockets

Powerful European Ariane rockets are used regularly to launch satellites into orbit around the Earth. They are the most successful commercial launchers. Any country can hire an Ariane to carry and release their satellites.

The European Ariane 4 blasting off from French Guyana in 1999. It launched an Indian telecommunications and weather satellite into geostationary orbit during its mission.

WHAT KEEPS A SATELLITE FROM FALLING BACK TO EARTH?

Gravity pulls constantly on a satellite. The balance of the gravitational force and the force pushing the satellite into space keeps it in orbit. Engineers calculate how fast the satellite must travel to stop gravity from pulling it back to Earth and to keep it from flying out of its Earth orbit.

The Ariane rocket is a three-stage rocket.

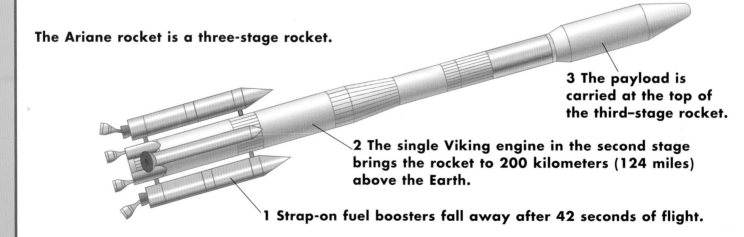

3 The payload is carried at the top of the third–stage rocket.

2 The single Viking engine in the second stage brings the rocket to 200 kilometers (124 miles) above the Earth.

1 Strap-on fuel boosters fall away after 42 seconds of flight.

Space probes

A SPACE PROBE IS AN unmanned spacecraft sent to investigate, gather and send back information from outer space. Space probes are different from satellites in that they are not placed in orbit, but sent to explore other parts of the solar system.

It was not until the 1970s that scientists developed the technology to explore the outer solar system. Deep-space probes have complicated computers and control systems. Even if a space probe is millions of miles away, exploring the outer solar system, it can be tracked from control centers on Earth.

PIONEER

In 1976, Pioneer 10 was the first of four spacecraft to fly to Jupiter. Pioneer 11 passed Jupiter and continued on to explore Saturn. Both vehicles are still being tracked and will be until about 2030.

VOYAGER 1 AND 2

The Voyager probes were launched by the United States in 1977 to fly into deep space. They made a detailed study of Jupiter in 1979, and then Saturn in 1980. From Saturn, Voyager 2 continued to the distant planets of Uranus, which it reached in 1986, and Neptune, which it reached in 1989. Both spacecraft are still travelling through outer space and will be tracked until about 2030.

The Voyager probes have sent back unique pictures of new moons orbiting Saturn. They also showed the complexity of the planet's many rings.

VENERA

In 1975, the Soviets launched Venera 9 and 10 to take photos of the surface of Venus. Capsules released by Venera 11 and 12 made landings on the surface of Venus in 1978.

VIKING 1 AND 2

The US Viking probes were launched in 1976 to investigate the planet Mars and to see if it could support life. The Viking probes sent pictures to Earth that gave scientists incredible views of the surface of the 'Red Planet'. Viking 2 continued to send back data from Mars until the mid-1990s.

ULYSSES

The US probe Ulysses was launched from the space shuttle US Discovery in 1990. Information returned by Ulysses assists scientists with their studies of the sun, solar winds and interstellar space.

THE HUBBLE SPACE TELESCOPE

The Hubble Space Telescope is a reflecting telescope that can see further and more clearly in space than any telescope on Earth. It was launched in 1990 from a NASA space shuttle and supplies astronomers with information about the universe. After launching, the main mirror in the Hubble Space Telescope was found to be faulty. In 1993, NASA sent another shuttle, the Endeavor, to repair the mirror. This mission was successful and the repairs were the most expensive in space history

MAGELLAN AND GALILEO

The US Galileo was launched in 1989 to explore and collect data about Jupiter and its satellites. It took six years of travel through the solar system to reach Jupiter's atmosphere. In 1990, the US Atlantis shuttle launched the probe Magellan, which orbited Venus and mapped the rocky landscape of Jupiter.

THE MARS PATHFINDER

In 1997, the US Mars Pathfinder probe landed on Mars. The journey to Mars took seven months. After a safe parachute landing, the spacecraft opened and a moon vehicle, Sojorner, unfolded its wheels and moved out to explore the surface of the planet.

The crew at the Jet Propulsion Laboratory in California look at the photos being sent back from Mars by the Mars Pathfinder, 1997.

The Hubble Space Telescope in orbit.

Future space flight

THE DAY WHEN ORDINARY people may travel into space is getting closer. Already there are a number of commercial companies offering bookings for the first tourist flights into space.

SPACE PLANES

There are **prototypes** and a great variety of designs for new airplanes that will fly around the world and into space. New materials, powerful engines and advanced wing shapes will assist aircraft to fly higher and faster.

The HOTOL (Horizontal Take-Off and Landing) rocket plane is a type of spaceplane designed to fly piggyback on a giant jet cargo plane to launch into space. HOTOLs are designed to fly through the atmosphere into space and glide back to Earth. Their engines are designed to work as turbofans in the atmosphere and as rockets in space. In the future, space planes may operate regular services to carry people and cargo in space and fly around the world in incredibly short times at speeds of Mach 5 or more.

These concept airplanes from the British Aerospace Agency are designed to shoot down missiles.

The International Space Station (ISS)

TODAY THE EXPLORATION of space has become a cooperative effort between many nations. A team of astronauts from different nations will work together to conduct experiments and research that may solve some of the Earth's environmental problems or find cures for diseases. It will provide living quarters for up to seven astronauts and scientists.

The International Space Station (ISS) is being assembled in space and is planned to be fully functional by 2004. The United States is mainly responsible for developing and operating it, but a combined team from Russia, Canada, Japan, Brazil and 11 other countries in the European Space Agency (Belgium, Denmark, France, Germany, Italy, Netherlands, Norway, Spain, Sweden, Switzerland and the United Kingdom) are also involved.

An artist's impression of what the International Space Station will one day look like.

SIZE OF THE ISS WHEN COMPLETED
Width: 110 meters (360.9 feet)
Length: 88 meters (288.7 feet)
Weight: 470,000 kilograms (519 tons)

GETTING TO AND FROM THE ISS

The Russian Soyuz spacecraft will take the first crew of three astronauts to the space station. The crew will spend three months aboard the ISS. The Soyuz spacecraft will remain docked with the station, providing an emergency return to Earth if needed by the crew. It will be replaced by a new spacecraft about every six months so there is always an escape route available. A new crew travelling aboard the space shuttle will relieve the first crew, who will return to Earth on the space shuttle.

CONSTRUCTING THE ISS

Astronauts will construct the space station in space, working in the searing heat and freezing cold. A new Canadian-built robotic arm will be used to move astronauts into work areas and as an overhead space crane to swing large space station modules into place. The astronauts will then bolt the pieces together using hand and power tools.

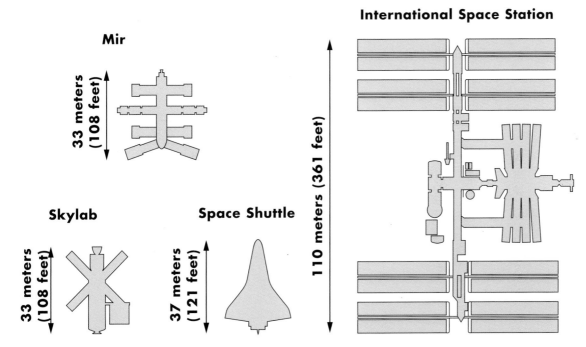

Mir — 33 meters (108 feet)

Skylab — 33 meters (108 feet)

Space Shuttle — 37 meters (121 feet)

International Space Station — 110 meters (361 feet)

The ISS will be four times larger than Mir and Skylab.

POWER FOR THE ISS

Huge solar panels, which cover almost 4,000 square meters (4,800 square yards), will collect the sun's energy and convert it into electrical energy. The energy will be stored in banks of batteries to be used in the laboratories and living quarters. Sixteen of the huge solar panels will make the wings on each side of the ISS.

Space Fact

The ISS will orbit at about 400 kilometers (249 miles) above the Earth.

Space flight timeline

1032 First war rockets propelled by gunpowder were used in China.

1944 Germany launches the first true modern rocket, V2, against England.

1957 USSR launches Sputnik 1, the world's first satellite.

1961 Lieutenant Yuri Gagarin (USSR), the first man in space, completes one orbit of the earth.

Alan Shepherd becomes the first American in space.

1962 John Glenn mans the first American flight to orbit the earth.

The first communications satellite, Telstar (USA), is launched.

1963 Valentina Tereshkova (USSR) becomes the first woman in space.

1964 Three cosmonauts orbit the earth in Voshkod 1.

1965 Alexei Leonov (USSR) makes the first space walk.

The first successful docking in space by US Gemini 6 and Gemini 7 is carried out.

1969 Neil Armstrong and Buzz Aldrin (USA) become the first men to walk on the moon.

1971 The first orbiting space station, Salyut (USSR), is launched.

The capsule from Soviet probe Mars 3 lands on Mars.

USSR's probe Mariner 9 is first to orbit Mars.

1973 Skylab, the United States' first space station, becomes operational.

1975 Apollo spacecraft (USA) docks with a Soyuz (USSR) spacecraft.

Soviet probe Venera 9 lands on Venus and photographs the planet's surface.

1976 The US Viking 1 sends photographs from Mars.

1977 The United States launches Voyagers 1 and 2 to Jupiter, Saturn, Uranus and Neptune.

1981 First flight of space shuttle Columbia with astronauts John Young and Robert Crippen (USA).

1983 US probe Pioneer 10 becomes the first spacecraft to travel beyond all the planets.

Dr Sally Ride is the first American woman to fly in space.

Spacelab, built by the European Space Agency, is first launched by space shuttle Columbia.

1984 US crew of space shuttle Challenger perform the first successful satellite recovery and repair mission.

1986 US space shuttle Challenger explodes shortly after launch, killing its crew of seven.

USSR launches the space station Mir, the first permanently occupied space station.

1990 The Hubble Space Telescope is launched by US Discovery.

1993 A space shuttle mission repairs the Hubble Space Telescope.

1994 US Ulysesses probe studies the sun's poles.

1995 US space shuttle Atlantis docks successfully with Soviet space station Mir.

Space probe Galileo arrives at Jupiter.

1997 US Mars Pathfinder lands on Mars.

1998 John Glenn, the first American to orbit the Earth, becomes the oldest person to travel in space.

1999 US and Russian missions begin assembly of the International Space Station.

2004 International Space Station due for completion.

Glossary

astronaut	a person who is trained to fly in a spacecraft
booster	a rocket used to provide extra thrust
cosmonaut	Russian word for a person who is trained to fly in a spacecraft
docking port	exit where two spacecraft are able to link and form an air-tight seal
gravity	the force of attraction between two large objects. The 'pull' of the Earth's force of gravity must be overcome to launch the shuttle into space
module	a section of a spacecraft that can be separated from other sections
NASA	the National Aeronautics and Space Administration, the United States space agency
orbit	1. (n) the flight path of a spacecraft or satellite as it circles the earth 2. (v) to travel around an object such as the Earth
orbiter	the only part of the space shuttle that travels into orbit and returns to Earth
payload	a commercial cargo, such as a satellite, carried on board a spacecraft. Customers can pay to send it into space
probe	an unmanned spacecraft
propulsion compartment	compartment that houses the engine
prototype	the first model of a new design or idea
reconnaissance	observing the enemies' forces or territories
satellite	a smaller object that orbits a larger one. The moon is a natural satellite of the earth. There are now many artificial satellites orbiting the Earth
thrust	the pushing force produced by a rocket engine

Index

Aldrin, Buzz   10, 30
animals   8
Apollo Lunar Program   7, 10–11, 16-17, 18–19, 30
Ariane rockets   24
Armstrong, Neil   10
astronauts   8, 10–11, 16, 18–19, 28–29, 30

booster rocket   12, 14, 24

Challenger   15, 30
Collins, Michael   10
Concorde   11
cosmonaut   9, 30

docking port   16–17, 30

HOTOL   27
Hubble Space Telescope   26, 30

Galileo   26, 30
Gargarin, Yuri   9, 30
geostationary orbit   21
Glenn, John   10, 30
Goddard, Robert   6, 30
gravity   11, 24

International Space Station   19, 28–29, 30

Leonov, Alexei   9, 30

Magellan   26
Mars fathfinder   26
Mir   16–17, 30
module   9, 10–11, 17, 29
moon   4, 7, 10–11, 16, 25, 26, 30
multi-stage rocket   6

NASA   7, 24, 26

orbit   5, 6, 8–9, 10–11, 12–13, 14–15, 16, 20–21, 22–23, 24, 25, 26, 28, 30
orbiter   12–13, 15

payload   24
Pioneer   25, 30
polar orbit   21
probe   12, 24, 25–26, 30
propulsion compartment   17
prototypes   27

reconnaissance   23
rockets   5, 6–7, 9, 10, 12–13, 14–15, 24, 27, 30

Salyut   16, 30
satellite   5, 12–13, 19, 20–21, 22–23, 24–25, 30
Saturn V   7, 10
Skylab   16, 30
space planes   27
space shuttle   12–13, 14–15, 17, 18, 24, 26, 28, 29, 30
space stations   16–17, 18–19, 28–29, 30
Sputnik 1   8 , 21, 30
Sputnik 2   8
sun   4, 17, 20, 26, 29, 30

Tereshkova, Valentina   7, 30
thrust   14, 19
Tsiolkovsky, Konstantin   6

Ulysses   26, 30

V-2 rocket   7
Venera   25
Viking 1 and 2   26, 30
Von Braun, Werner   7
Vostok 1   9

woll

THOMAS CRANE PUBLIC LIBRARY

3 1641 00454 1573

WOLLASTON